The NeverGirls

Pixie Puzzles, Games, and More!

Written by Andrea Posner-Sanchez
Based on the series by Kiki Thorpe
Illustrated by Jana Christy

A STEPPING STONE BOOK™
Random House 🏠 New York

randomhouse.com/kids

ISBN 978-0-7364-3152-1

Printed in the United States of America

10 9 8 7 6 5 4 3

Meet the Girls

These four friends share an amazing adventure! Look up, down, across, backward, and diagonally to find their names in the puzzle.

GABBY   KATE   LAINEY   MIA

```
Y E B B L P T K
N L A I N E Y B
I C T E E W S Y
T B K O I A K G
M I A Y B I A L
N O S C G B T N
L W G M B I E G
E L A Y K M O L
```

See page 231 for the answer.

3

Never Girls Trivia

1. What game were Kate, Lainey, and Mia playing when Gabby discovered a fairy?

    A) Soccer

    B) Hide-and-Seek

    C) Hopscotch

    D) Softball

2. What kind of birds did Lainey see flying over the backyard?

    A) Owls

    B) Macaws

    C) Flamingos

    D) Penguins

3. Who is Gabby's sister?

    A) Lainey

    B) Kate

    C) Prilla

    D) Mia

See page 231 for the answers.

Fairy-Speak

Use the reverse alphabet code to find out what Prilla says to Gabby.

"XOZK RU BLF YVORVEV RM UZRIRVH!"

"_C L A P_ _I F_ _Y O U_
_Y O U B E_____ ____
_____!"

A = Z	N = M
B = Y	O = L
C = X	P = K
D = W	Q = J
E = V	R = I
F = U	S = H
G = T	T = G
H = S	U = F
I = R	V = E
J = Q	W = D
K = P	X = C
L = O	Y = B
M = N	Z = A

See page 231 for the answer.

Name Game

What do the fairies call people from the mainland? To find out, replace each letter with the one that comes after it in the alphabet.

BKTLRHDR

_ _ _ _ _ _ _ _

See page 231 for the answer.

welcome to Never Land

Imagine you're in Never Land.
Draw yourself in the scene below.

Fit for a Fairy

Tinker Bell's workshop is located inside a common Clumsy item. Connect the dots to see what it is.

See page 231 for the answer.

A Special Friend

Before Tinker Bell got to know Kate, Mia, Lainey, and Gabby, there was only one human she liked. To find out who it is, follow the lines and write each letter in the correct box.

N P T A E P E R

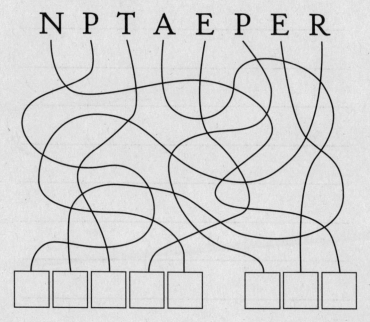

See page 231 for the answer.

9

Dream Time

The first time the girls saw Pixie Hollow, they felt as if they were dreaming. What is your most marvelous dream? Write about it here.

_____

_____

_____

_____

_____

_____

_____

_____

_____

_____

A Royal Meeting

Gabby is honored to meet Queen Clarion.
Help lead her through the maze.

See page 232 for the answer.

Message from the Queen

Leaf Lettering is a secret fairy alphabet. Follow the code to read a message from Queen Clarion.

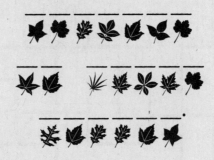

See page 232 for the answer.

First Fairy Feast

The fairies serve delicious—but tiny—food to the girls. Can you fit the food words into the puzzle?

CAKE   BREAD   WALNUTS

CHEESE   STRAWBERRIES

See page 232 for the answer.

Choose a word

Find the best word from the list below to complete each sentence.

BLINK   CLOUD   DAISY   HOME
PAPER   PINE   RAINCOAT   ROSE
SCARF   TUTU   WINK

1. The fairies all live in the _____ Tree.

2. Queen Clarion wears a gown made of

_____ petals.

3. Prilla travels to the mainland on a

_____.

4. Gabby likes to wear a _____ and

wings.

See page 232 for the answers.

Home, Sweet Home

Can you find these words that have to do with the Home Tree? Look up, down, across, backward, and diagonally.

BRANCH   KNOTHOLE   MAPLE

ROOM   TRUNK   WINDOW

```
A I M T E W W B J R
H L B A Z O M R A E
W K U D P A O H V D
S N O I W L J B I R
I O R F U I E Y X F
J T I L Q N L A S U
T H C N A R B O K W
V O D O K Y H Q C O
R L F T R O O M R D
M E W Y X T S B E N
A U S C D M Z A L I
T R U N K I H E E W
```

See page 233 for the answer.

Tiny Things

Mia and Kate are amazed to see the tiny items in the fairies' tearoom. Seashells are used as plates, and flower petals are used as napkins. What do you think the fairies could use these items for? Write some ideas beneath each one.

ACORN CAP

_____

_____

_____

PEBBLE

_____

_____

_____

PINE NEEDLE

_____

_____

_____

FEATHER

_____

_____

_____

Mind Your Manners

Cross out all the letters in the word FAIRY and write the remaining letters on the line below.

FFAYCIRFYU
AFYITAEFRI

— — — —

Why should you never use this word to describe a fairy?

_____

_____

_____

_____

_____

_____

A = Z	
B = Y	
C = X	
D = W	
E = V	
F = U	
G = T	
H = S	
I = R	
J = Q	
K = P	
L = O	
M = N	
N = M	
O = L	
P = K	
Q = J	
R = I	
S = H	
T = G	
U = F	
V = E	
W = D	
X = C	
Y = B	
Z = A	

Mind Your Manners 2

Fairies don't apologize the way Clumsies do. Use the reverse alphabet code to find out what fairies say instead of "I'm sorry."

"R'W UOB YZXPDZIW RU R XLFOW."

"___ ___ ____

_____ __

__ _____."

18

See page 233 for the answer.

On the Run

Uh-oh! Kate accidentally lets the dairy mice out. Which path will lead the mice back to the barn?

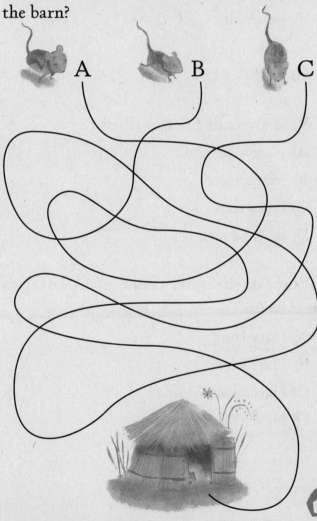

A   B   C

See page 233 for the answer.

Pixie Hollow Trivia

1. What is the fairy dust mill made of?

   A) pinecones

   B) peach pits

   C) rocks

   D) bricks

2. What are male fairies called?

   A) pigeon men

   B) parrot men

   C) robin men

   D) sparrow men

3. Where do the water-talent fairies sail their leaf-boats?

   A) Fairy Pond

   B) Pixie River

   C) Havendish Stream

   D) Never Land Brook

See page 233 for the answers.

Find the Match

Which two pictures are identical?

A

B

C

D

E

F

See page 233 for the answer.

Fairy Dust Facts

Which three statements are true?

1. Fairy dust is stored in pumpkin canisters.
2. Fairies can help themselves to as much fairy dust as they like.
3. Fairies can fly without fairy dust—but only for very short distances.
4. Terence is allergic to fairy dust.
5. Fairy dust smells like popcorn.
6. Fairy dust makes fairies sparkle.

See page 233 for the answers.

Home Away from Home

When they stay in Pixie Hollow, the girls share a lovely room under a willow tree. To find out what is used to light their lanterns, follow the lines and write each letter in the correct box.

L S I F E F I E R

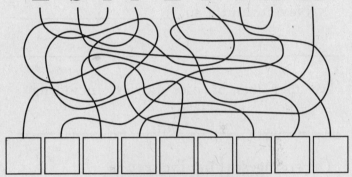

See page 233 for the answer.

Fairy Mail

Mia writes a note for Prilla to deliver to her parents. Pretend you are visiting Never Land. What would you write home about? Finish the letter any way you like.

Dear _____ ,

    Never Land is so _____

_____ .

I've met lots of nice fairies, including

_____ and _____ .

The strangest thing I've seen is _____

_____

_____ .

I really love the _____

_____

_____ .

Dear Mami and Papi,
How are you? We are fine. We are
visiting in Never Land. It's nice here.
Please tell the other moms don't worry.
Love, Mia Gabby Lainey Kate

I've had the most fun _____

_____

_____

_____.

The thing I miss most from home is

_____

_____

_____

_____.

Love, _____

A Royal Message

Follow the leaf code to read a message from Queen Clarion.

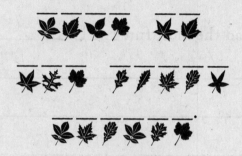

See page 233 for the answer.

Have a Seat

Connect the dots to see what the fairies sit on in the fairy circle.

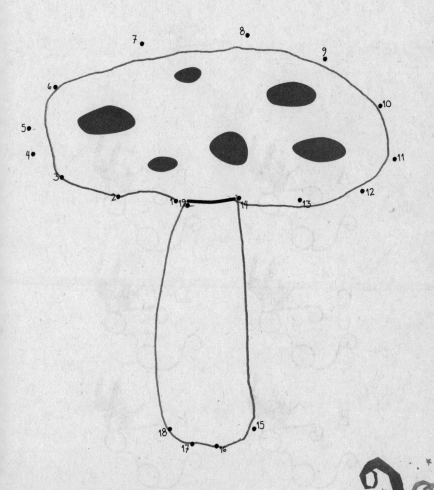

See page 234 for the answer.

Seeing Clearly

Skye is a seeing talent. Can you see which shadow matches her picture exactly?

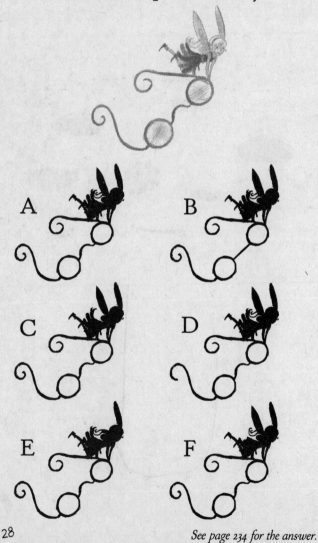

A

B

C

D

E

F

See page 234 for the answer.

A Big Request

What does Kate ask to do when the girls are told they only have one more day in Pixie Hollow? Unscramble the words to find out.

"EW TNAW OT

ENLAR OT LYF."

"__ __ _____ ___

_____ __ _____."

See page 234 for the answer.

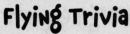

Flying Trivia

1. How much fairy dust is poured over each girl to make her fly?

    A) one cupful

    B) a sprinkling

    C) one thimbleful

    D) a teaspoonful

2. What does Kate accidentally bump into the first time she flies?

    A) a flamingo

    B) a sparrow man

    C) a tree branch

    D) a flagpole

3. What does Tink do when the girls land in Havendish Stream?

    A) covers her eyes

    B) laughs

    C) flies for help

    D) jumps in

See page 234 for the answers.

we Can Fly!

Help lead Lainey through the maze so she can fly with Mia.

See page 234 for the answer.

Light as Air

It helps to think of light items such as feathers, clouds, and dandelion fluff when trying to fly. How many other light things can you think of? Write them here:

_____

_____

_____

_____

_____

Now think of some super-heavy items. Write them here:

_____

_____

_____

_____

_____

_____

Meet Vidia

Start at the arrow and, going clockwise around the circle, write every other letter in order on the lines below to complete the sentence.

Vidia is a ___ ___ ___ ___ -

___ ___ ___ ___ ___ ___

___ ___ ___ ___ ___ .

See page 234 for the answer.

Dust Holder

What does Vidia give Kate to fill with fairy dust? Connect the dots to find out.

2•   •3

•4

1•

17•

5•

16•   •6

15•

14•   •7

13•   •8

12•

11•   •9

10•

See page 235 for the answer.

Look! Up in the Sky!

Unscramble the letters to discover things that fly. Then write the letters in the circles in order on the lines below to name a dust-talent sparrow man.

TLTUBYFRE

☐ ☐ ◯ ☐ ◯ ☐ ☐ ☐ ☐

FYIRA

☐ ☐ ☐ ◯ ☐

TIEK

☐ ☐ ☐ ◯

RAEPNLIA

☐ ☐ ☐ ☐ ☐ ☐ ◯ ☐

OTIRHECPLE

☐ ☐ ☐ ☐ ◯ ☐ ☐ ☐ ◯ ☐

— — — — — — — — —

See page 235 for the answers.

Tinker Time

Look up, down, across, and diagonally to find these words.

HAMMER   METAL   ~~PANS~~

POTS   ~~TINK~~   ~~WORKSHOP~~

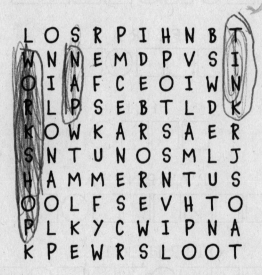

```
L O S R P I H N B T
W N E M D P V S I
O I A F C E O I W N
R L P S E B T L D K
K O W A R S A E R
S N T U N O S M L J
H A M M E R N T U S
O O L F S E V H T O
P L K Y C W I P N A
K P E W R S L O O T
```

See page 235 for the answer.

Feathered Friend

Beck and Tink search for Kate on the back of a bird. To find out what kind of bird it is, follow the lines and write each letter in the correct box.

N S G I R L A T

See page 235 for the answer.

what's the weather?

Rain is a weather-talent fairy who uses strange words. Luckily, Skye understands what she means. Try to match what Rain says with Skye's interpretation.

1. "Mark is aflay."
2. "Cold highwilds drove the isle mainlandish."
3. "Could be as soon as sun-twixt."

A) "It might be between the next sunrise and sunset."
B) "It's time to go."
C) "Never Land rode the waves all the way to the mainland."

See page 235 for the answers.

Mind Your Manners 3

What do fairies say instead of "good-bye"? To find out, replace each letter with the one that comes after it in the alphabet.

"EKX RZEDKX!"

"_____ _____!"

See page 235 for the answer.

Pattern Path

Follow the pattern up, down, left, and right (but not diagonally) to make it through the maze.

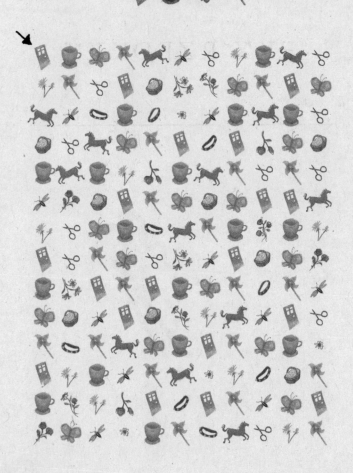

See page 236 for the answer.

Talking with Tink

What do you think Tinker Bell and Kate are saying to each other? Write your ideas in the speech bubbles.

Get wordy

How many words can you make from the letters in THE SPACE BETWEEN?

_____   _____

_____   _____

_____   _____

_____   _____

_____   _____

_____   _____

_____   _____

                            _____

                            _____

                            _____

                            _____

                            _____

See page 236 for the answers.

Furry Racer

Fawn loves to ride around on her squirrel friend. Which shadow matches the picture exactly?

See page 236 for the answer.

Talk to the Animals

Fawn teaches Lainey how to speak Mouse and Chickadee. Look up, down, across, backward, and diagonally to find these animal sounds in the puzzle.

CHIRP   HISS   MEOW   MOO

NEIGH   OINK

```
R  H  E  O  A  M  P  E
N  E  I  G  H  C  O  R
G  P  M  L  Y  W  F  O
N  O  I  N  K  B  G  N
W  A  C  L  H  J  A  I
O  S  C  H  I  R  P  C
E  O  L  U  S  W  H  E
M  S  H  P  S  A  O  O
```

See page 236 for the answer.

High Praise

Fawn says something to Lainey that makes her very happy. To find out what it is, fill in the missing vowels.

"Y __ __ ' R __

B __ C __ M __ NG

__ R __ __ L

__ N __ M __ L-T __ L __ NT

C L __ M S Y."

See page 237 for the answer.

Crazy About Animals

If you could have any animal as a pet, what would it be? _____

_____

What would you name your pet? _____

_____

What tricks would you teach your pet?

_____

_____

_____

If you could talk to animals, what would you say? _____

_____

_____

_____

What animal would your parents not
want in the house? _____
_____
_____

_____

_____

_____

_____

_____

_____

_____

_____

_____

_____

_____

Leaf-Boat Racers

Follow the paths to see which water-talent fairy reaches the end of the stream.

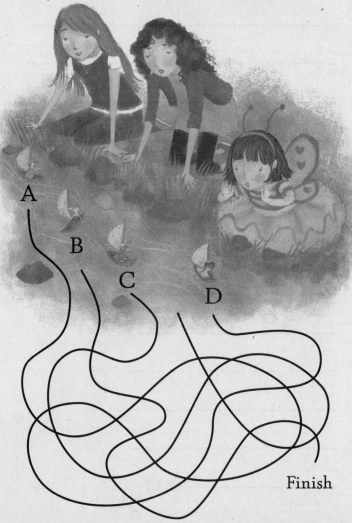

A

B

C

D

Finish

See page 237 for the answer.

Never Land Souvenirs

Each girl decides to take one item home with her to the mainland. Match each girl with the item she chooses.

Mia ___
Kate ___
Gabby ___
Lainey ___

A) a daisy garland to wear as a crown
B) a fan made from daisy petals and pine needles
C) a mouse-herder's lasso to wear as a bracelet
D) a kaleidoscope with a dewdrop lens

See page 237 for the answers.

A Special Gift

What does Terence give the girls? Unscramble the words to find out.

NOE CINPH

FO RAYFI

SDUT AHCE

___ _____

__ _____

_____ ____

See page 237 for the answer.

A Lot of Tink

How many pictures of Tinker Bell can you spot?

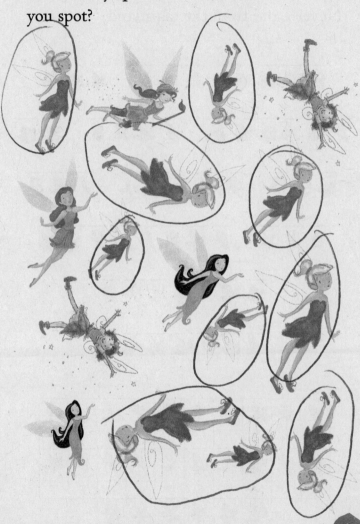

See page 237 for the answer.

Magical Directions

Follow the leaf code to learn how to get to Never Land from the mainland.

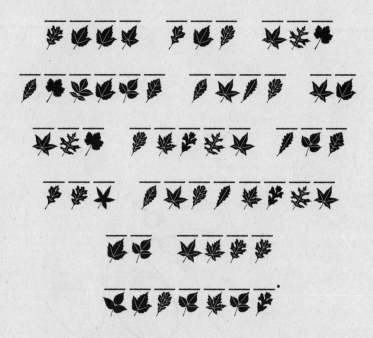

See page 237 for the answer.

Mind Reader

What do you suppose Fawn is thinking?
Write it inside the thought bubble.

Bingo Is His Name-o

Mia is excited to see her cat. How many times can you find the name BINGO in the puzzle? Look up, down, across, backward, and diagonally.

```
G  B  B  O  N  O  B
O  I  O  I  B  N  I
B  N  G  B  N  I  N
O  G  N  I  B  G  G
I  O  G  O  I  I  O
B  I  N  G  O  B  N
I  N  B  I  N  G  O
```

See page 237 for the answer.

Nice Mice Names

The dairy mice in Pixie Hollow have names like Thistledown, Cloverseed, and Milkweed. Make your own compound-word names by choosing words from column A and combining them with words from column B. Write the names on the lines below.

Column A	Column B
Sugar	Breeze
Pansy	Light
Beetle	Root
Tulip	Blade
Windy	Nut
Petal	Stem
Sandy	Grass
Silver	Land
Feather	Corn
Shimmer	Sun

_____

_____

_____

_____

Big House

Fawn peeks inside the Clumsy house and sees the items listed below. Can you fit the words into the puzzle? Some letters are already filled in.

BOOKS   CHAIRS   LAMPS

SHOES   TABLE

See page 237 for the answer.

BOW-WOW

What does Lainey say to the barking dog?
Use the reverse alphabet code to find out.

"WLM'G YV HL
TILFXSB. R'N BLFI
UIRVMW."

" _ _ _ _ ' _   _ _   _ _

_ _ _ _ _ _ _ .   _ ' _

_ _ _ _   _ _ _ _ _ _ ."

A = Z	
B = Y	
C = X	
D = W	
E = V	
F = U	
G = T	
H = S	
I = R	
J = Q	
K = P	
L = O	
M = N	
N = M	
O = L	
P = K	
Q = J	
R = I	
S = H	
T = G	
U = F	
V = E	
W = D	
X = C	
Y = B	
Z = A	

See page 237 for the answer.

57

Mouse Catcher

What does Lainey's mother use to chase the mouse out of the kitchen? To find out, follow the lines and write each letter in the correct box.

O A M B O R

See page 238 for the answer.

A Tasty Treat

Lead the mouse to the cheese.

See page 238 for the answer.

Mainland Trivia

1. How does Fawn leave Never Land and arrive on the mainland?

   A) on a cloud

   B) in Kate's pocket

   C) on a blink

   D) through a hollow fig tree

2. What does Fawn notice about the grass in Mia's yard?

   A) It's greener than the grass in Pixie Hollow.

   B) Every blade is snipped off at the exact same height.

   C) It tickles her wings.

   D) It needs to be watered.

3. What kind of animal does Lainey see every time she walks to Mia's house?

   A) a hedgehog

   B) a rat

   C) a goat

   D) a dog

See page 238 for the answers.

Choose a Word 2

Find the best word to complete each sentence below.

SHOE   DOOR   BRUSH

FURRY   PLASTIC   BELLS

LEASHES   FENCE   CUT   HAT

1. Bingo and Milkweed both have

_____ around their necks.

2. Lainey's mom tells her to _____

her hair.

3. Fawn escapes back to Never Land

through a gap in the _____.

4. Lainey puts Milkweed in a _____

box.

See page 238 for the answers.

Cat Confusion

Bingo isn't sure what Fawn is, but he makes two guesses. To see Bingo's first guess, cross out all the letters in the word FAWN and write the remaining letters on the lines below.

WNBFAINWAFRANDW

—— —— —— —— ——

Now replace each letter below with the one that comes before it in the alphabet to see Bingo's second guess.

ESBHPOGMZ

—— —— —— —— —— —— —— —— ——

See page 238 for the answers.

Fruity Fun

Fawn tosses a raspberry at Bingo to get the cat to stop chasing her. Can you fit the fruit words listed below into the puzzle?

BANANA   GRAPE   LEMON
ORANGE   RASPBERRY

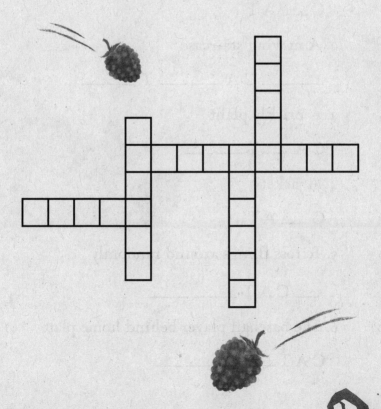

See page 238 for the answer.

CAT!

Every answer in this puzzle is a word that contains the letters C, A, and T, in that order. Read the clues and see how many you can guess.

1. Talk

   C __ A T

2. A moving staircase

   __ __ C A __ __ T __ __

3. A prickly plant

   C A __ T __ __

4. A jacket

   C __ A T

5. To toss things around randomly

   __ C A T __ __ __

6. The baseball player behind home plate

   C A T __ __ __ __

See page 238 for the answers.

An unwelcome Guest

Bingo arrives at the Home Tree and chases the fairies. Help lead them safely through the maze. Be sure to avoid the cat!

FINISH

See page 239 for the answer.

Fairy Dots

With a friend, take turns drawing a line to connect two dots below. When a line you draw completes a box, give yourself one point. If there's a fairy in the box, give yourself two points. When no more boxes can be made, the player with more points wins.

Play again!

A = 1	
B = 2	# Scat!
C = 3	How do Dulcie and the kitchen fairies get
D = 4	Bingo out of the Home Tree kitchen? Use
E = 5	the number code to complete the sentences
F = 6	and find the answers.
G = 7	
H = 8	They bang on
I = 9	
J = 10	16-15-20-19 1-14-4
K = 11	16-1-14-19
L = 12	
M = 13	__ __ __ __ __ __ __
N = 14	
O = 15	__ __ __ __ .
P = 16	
Q = 17	They throw
R = 18	
S = 19	16-5-16-16-5-18-3-15-
T = 20	18-14-19
U = 21	
V = 22	
W = 23	__ __ __ __ __ __ __ __ __ __ __ .
X = 24	
Y = 25	
Z = 26	

See page 239 for the answers.

Which Mouse?

In what way does Milkweed look different from the other dairy mice? To find out, start at the arrow and, going clockwise around the circle, write every other letter in order on the lines below.

__ ___ _

_____ __

____ ____.

See page 239 for the answer.

Breakfast Time

What does Lainey feed Milkweed for breakfast? To find out, cross out all the letters in the word YUM and write the remaining letters on the lines below.

U Y W M M Y A U

F U M Y Y F M U

M L Y M U M E U Y

— — — — — —

70

See page 239 for the answer.

Out of Order

The words in each vertical column go into the spaces directly below them, but not in the order they appear. When they're placed correctly, you'll be able to read what Lainey is saying to her friends.

IN	THAT	HOME	NEVER
STRANGE	MY	TURNED	UP
DON'T	MOUSE	A	IT'S
LAND	YOU	THINK	
			?

See page 239 for the answer.

Birds of a Feather

The girls are surprised to see a flamingo in the yard. Can you find all the bird names listed in the puzzle below? Look up, down, across, backward, and diagonally.

DOVE   FLAMINGO   OSTRICH

PARROT   PIGEON

```
P E N V L T T F O
I T O W G P D S I
G P A R R O T B M
E C H V D R M E R
O S D A I O Y K G
N T Y C A J F C V
E M H V G K L E S
D A G J L S B V A
F L A M I N G O J
S R T D C R L D F
```

See page 239 for the answer.

Follow the Flamingo

Can you get through the maze by following the path of flamingos that are only facing right? You can move up, down, left, and right (but not diagonally).

See page 240 for the answer.

Petal Pushers

Kate chases the flamingo through Mia's mother's flowers. Can you unscramble these flower names?

SEOR

__ __ __ __

AYDIS

__ __ __ __ __

UPATNIE

__ __ __ __ __ __ __

ITLPU

__ __ __ __ __

GMADOILR

__ __ __ __ __ __ __ __

See page 240 for the answers.

Poor Dooley!

Fawn rescues Dooley from being batted around by Bingo. Follow the leaf code to see what Dooley tells his friends about his ordeal.

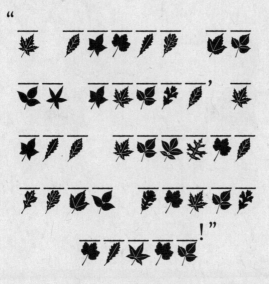

See page 240 for the answer.

TWIN TINKS

Which two pictures of Tinker Bell are exactly alike?

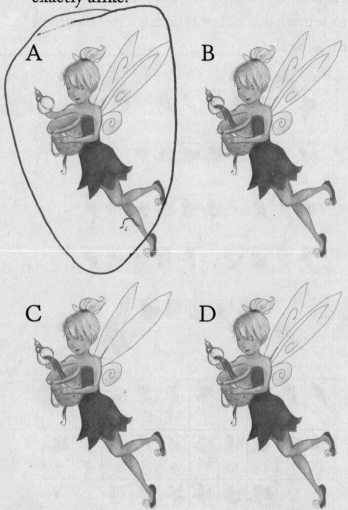

A

B

C

D

See page 240 for the answer.

Holy Moley!

Tinker Bell realizes there's a hole between Never Land and the mainland. But just because something has a hole in it doesn't mean it's broken. Some items, such as watering cans and sneakers, need holes. How many other items with holes can you think of? List them here.

_____

_____

_____

_____

_____

_____

_____

_____

_____

_____

Awnk!

Lainey wants to try to speak Flamingo. Lead her through the maze to get to the bird.

See page 240 for the answer.

Gotcha!

What does Kate use to catch the flamingo?
Circle it.

A 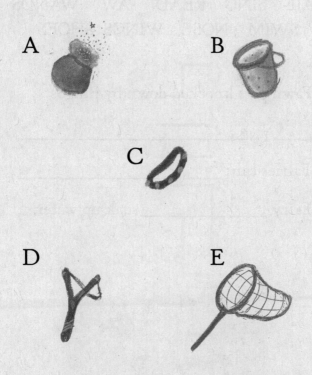 B

C

D   E

Choose a word 3

Find the best word below to complete each sentence.

TAIL SING READ PAW WANDS
SWIM NOSE WINGS SHOES

1. Fawn gets knocked down by Bingo's

_____.

2. Fairies can't _____.

3. Fairy _____ soak up water.

See page 240 for the answers.

Splash!

What does Tink lose in the stream?
Use the number code to find out.

8 - 5 - 18

19 - 12 - 9 - 14 - 7 - 19 - 8 - 15 - 20

__ __ __

__ __ __ __ __ __ __ __ __

A = 1	
B = 2	
C = 3	
D = 4	
E = 5	
F = 6	
G = 7	
H = 8	
I = 9	
J = 10	
K = 11	
L = 12	
M = 13	
N = 14	
O = 15	
P = 16	
Q = 17	
R = 18	
S = 19	
T = 20	
U = 21	
V = 22	
W = 23	
X = 24	
Y = 25	
Z = 26	

See page 240 for the answer.

Pattern Path 2

Follow the pattern up, down, left, and right (but not diagonally) to make it through the maze.

See page 241 for the answer.

Tink's Little Habit

What does Tinker Bell often do when she is thinking? Unscramble the words to find out.

HSE GSTU

NO RHE

ASBGN

___ ____

__ ___

_____.

See page 241 for the answer.

Special Friends

Friends come in all shapes and sizes—some are even fairy-sized!

Who is your best friend?_____

_____

How long have you been friends?_____

Where did you meet?_____

_____

List some things you and your best friend

have in common: _____

_____

_____

List some things that are different about

you and your best friend:_____

_____

_____

What do you like most about your best friend?_____

_____

_____

What is your favorite thing to do together?

_____

_____

_____

_____

_____

Get wordy 2

How many words can you make from the letters in A DANDELION WISH?

_____   _____

_____   _____

_____   _____

_____   _____

_____   _____

_____   _____

_____   _____

_____   _____

                                        _____

  _____

  _____

  _____

  _____

Four real girls in a fairy's world.

the NeVeR GiRls

a dandelion wish

Kiki Thorpe

See page 241 for the answers.

Fairy Portrait

Gabby drew this picture of Tinker Bell.
Draw your own fairy portrait here.

Calling All Parents

What do Mia and Gabby call their parents? To find out, begin at the M and write the letters in order as they appear from left to right on the lines below.

M

A M

I A N

D P A P I

___ ___ ___ ___

___ ___ ___

___ ___ ___ ___

See page 241 for the answer.

The Thinkers

What are Gabby and Mia thinking about?
Write your ideas in the thought bubbles.

Secret Passage

Never Land is just on the other side of the fence in Mia's yard. Can you find these words in the puzzle? Look up, down, across, backward, and diagonally.

BOARD   FENCE   GAP   NAIL

WOOD   YARD

```
N O P F I Y O N B
G A H S E L G A P
O B I V Q N T Y N
E W O L J S C U V
Y P C O H B R E A
A F I G D O S L D
R B N Y C A L V B
D O O W Y R G F O
E N S M F D U J A
```

See page 241 for the answer.

Under Construction

The fairies are repairing their footbridge. Use the reverse alphabet code to find out how it broke, according to Tinker Bell.

"DV GSRMP YRMTL
NFHG SZEV
HNZHSVW RG DSVM
SV DZH XSZHRMT
UZRIRVH."

" __ __ __   __ __ __ __ __

__ __ __ __ __   __ __ __ __

__ __ __ __ __   __ __ __ __ __ __

__ __   __ __ __ __ __   __ __ __

__ __ __   __ __ __ __ __ __ __ __

__ __ __ __ __ __ __ __ ."

Right column code key
A = Z
B = Y
C = X
D = W
E = V
F = U
G = T
H = S
I = R
J = Q
K = P
L = O
M = N
N = M
O = L
P = K
Q = J
R = I
S = H
T = G
U = F
V = E
W = D
X = C
Y = B
Z = A

See page 241 for the answer.

Talent Matching

Can you match each fairy with her talent?

1. Prilla   ___
2. Tinker Bell   ___
3. Rosetta   ___
4. Dulcie   ___
5. Rain   ___
6. Fawn   ___

A) animal talent
B) weather talent
C) clapping talent
D) pots-and-pans talent
E) baking talent
F) garden talent

See page 242 for the answers.

All About Rosetta

Circle the facts that are true.

1. Rosetta doesn't like the smell of roses.
2. Rosetta's house is made from a gourd.
3. Rosetta has red hair.
4. Rosetta is a water-talent fairy.
5. Rosetta can hear the secrets inside a seed.

See page 242 for the answers.

Best Dressed

Rosetta loves trying on dresses. Can you design some new ones for her? Draw them here.

Making the Bed

Mia brings Rosetta to her room and regrets that she hadn't made her bed that morning. Every answer in this puzzle is a word that contains the letters B, E, and D, in that order. Read the clues and see how many you can figure out.

1. A sandwich has two slices of this:
   B __ E __ D

2. When you have a cut, it might do this:
   B __ E __ D

3. This can be on a necklace or bracelet:
   B E __ D

4. Stolen:
   __ __ B __ E D

5. Drooled:
   __ __ __ B __ E __ __ D

See page 242 for the answers.

Fairy-Sized

Rosetta feels right at home in Mia's dollhouse. All the scrambled words below are items found in the dollhouse. Try to unscramble them all.

1. ONPYCA DBE _____
2. SRSEEDR _____
3. CCUHO _____
4. ENOV _____
5. ALPM _____
6. LTEBA _____
7. PWOLLI _____
8. HCRAI _____
9. ITRCAUN _____
10. UGR _____

See page 242 for the answers.

Fashion Line

Lead Rosetta through the maze by following this dress 👗 up, down, and diagonally.

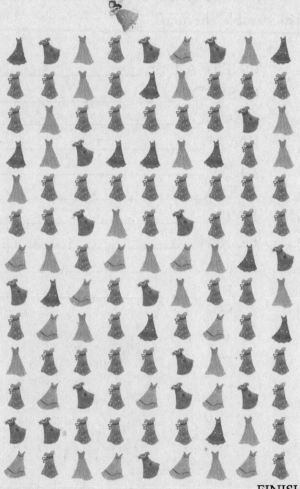

FINISH

See page 242 for the answer.

A Clue

What does Mia see on the ground near the fence that helps her realize Gabby went to Never Land? To find out, replace each letter below with the one that comes after it in the alphabet.

FZAAX'R

RVDZSRGHQS

__ __ __ __ __ '__

__ __ __ __ __ __ __ __ __ __ __

See page 242 for the answer.

In a Fix

Oh, no! Mia's dad fixes the fence! Why is this bad? Fill in the missing vowels to complete the sentences below.

R__S__TT__ __S

ST__CK __N TH__

M____NL__ND.

G__BBY __S ST__CK

__N N__V__R L__ND.

See page 242 for the answers.

Gathering Sunbeams

Iridessa is making and collecting sunbeam balls. Which path will lead her to the basket of sunbeam balls?

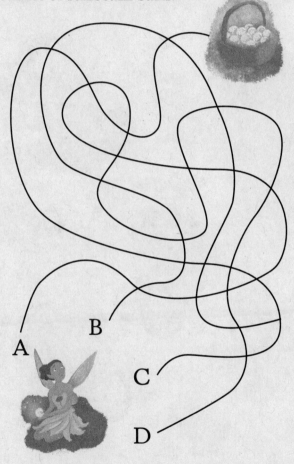

See page 242 for the answer.

The One and Only Gabby

Find and circle the picture of Gabby that matches this one.

See page 242 for the answer.

Tink's Report

What does Tinker Bell tell Queen Clarion? Use the number code to find out.

"20-8-5

16-15-18-20-1-12

8-1-19

22-1-14-9-19-8-5-4!"

" ___ ___ ___

___ ___ ___ ___ ___ ___

___ ___ ___

___ ___ ___ ___ ___ ___ ___ !"

A = 1	
B = 2	
C = 3	
D = 4	
E = 5	
F = 6	
G = 7	
H = 8	
I = 9	
J = 10	
K = 11	
L = 12	
M = 13	
N = 14	
O = 15	
P = 16	
Q = 17	
R = 18	
S = 19	
T = 20	
U = 21	
V = 22	
W = 23	
X = 24	
Y = 25	
Z = 26	

See page 243 for the answer.

Shocking News

What does Rosetta do when she learns that the way back to Never Land is gone? To find out, follow the lines and write each letter in the correct box.

T F S A E S H I N

See page 243 for the answer.

Snack Time

Mia gives Rosetta a drop of root beer and something crunchy to eat. To name the snack, complete the maze and write the letters that form the correct path in the blanks.

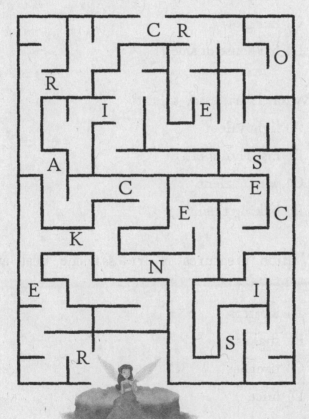

_____ _____ _____ _____ _____ _____ _____

Trivia: Iridessa

1. What is stronger about Iridessa than with other fairies?

   A) her muscles

   B) her perfume

   C) her glow

   D) her sense of smell

2. What is Iridessa's talent?

   A) light talent

   B) fast-flying talent

   C) water talent

   D) baking talent

3. Which creatures is Iridessa the best at gathering?

   A) lobsters

   B) snakes

   C) fireflies

   D) mice

See page 243 for the answers.

Make a Wish

What does Gabby think happens when you wish on a dandelion? To find out, start at the arrow and, going counterclockwise around the picture, write the letters in the blanks below.

__ _____ _____

____ _____ ____

_____ __ _____

_____.

See page 243 for the answer.

Something in the Air

Gabby and Iridessa discover thousands of fireflies, but they soon turn off their lights and fly away.

To find out what scares the fireflies, draw lines connecting them to form letters.

See page 243 for the answer.

Forest words

Can you fit the words below into the puzzle?

BRANCHES   FOREST   GRASS

LEAF   TREE

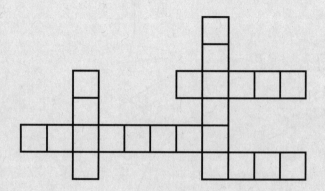

See page 243 for the answer.

Meet the Neighbor

Mia goes into the neighbor's garden to find Rosetta. To learn the neighbor's name, follow the lines and write each letter in the correct box.

V A M R E Y P S

See page 243 for the answer.

Garden Woes

Rosetta is disturbed by Mrs. Peavy's overgrown, messy garden. Follow the leaf code to see what she tells Mia.

See page 244 for the answer.

Flower Dots

With a friend, take turns drawing a line to connect two dots below. When a line you draw completes a box, give yourself one point. If there's a flower in the box, give yourself two points. When no more boxes can be made, the player with more points wins.

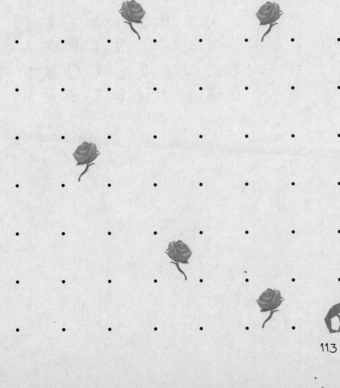

From Bad . . .

Look up, down, across, backward, and diagonally to find these words in the puzzle.

BROWN   DIRT   OVERGROWN

WEEDS   WILTED

```
D T B W O S V E R D
A I G R D E T L I W
W X R V W P L S G L
E D S T E O M Y B I
E N B U X J A E R T
D T L E F N I P O A
S O V E R G R O W N
G B R Y W D E S N U
```

See page 244 for the answer.

... to Beautiful

More words to search for! Look up, down, across, backward, and diagonally to find them in the puzzle.

BLOOM   BLOSSOM   GREEN

SPROUT   WATER

```
M O N G W O T P G Y
B L O S S O M I R A
W F N C Z V O S E T
G A W P M C O H E U
E E T I H O L A N O
J T S E G E B J X R
A M T I R X W E W P
N S O A U S S B A S
```

See page 244 for the answer.

A = 1
B = 2
C = 3
D = 4
E = 5
F = 6
G = 7
H = 8
I = 9
J = 10
K = 11
L = 12
M = 13
N = 14
O = 15
P = 16
Q = 17
R = 18
S = 19
T = 20
U = 21
V = 22
W = 23
X = 24
Y = 25
Z = 26

Quiet, Please

What does Rosetta say when she hears the lawn mower? Use the number code to find out.

"9-20-'19   12-15-21-4-5-18

20-8-1-14   1

2-21-12-12-6-18-15-7

23-9-20-8   1

2-5-12-12-25-1-3-8-5!"

" _ _ _ _ ' _ _   _ _ _ _ _ _ _

_ _ _ _   _ _

_ _ _ _ _ _ _ _

_ _ _ _   _ _

_ _ _ _ _ _ _ _ _ !"

116

See page 244 for the answer.

Look Sharp!

Which shadow matches the picture exactly?

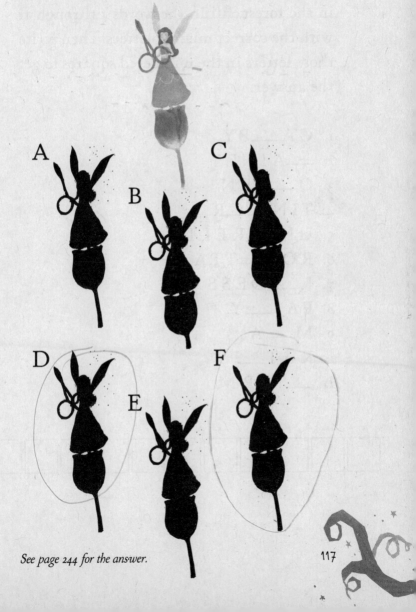

A

B

C

D

E

F

See page 244 for the answer.

Forest Nibble

To find out what Gabby and Iridessa eat in the forest, fill in the words 1 through 11 with the correct missing letters. Then write those letters in the numbered squares to get the answer.

1. G A __ B Y
2. __ A I N E Y
3. Q __ E E N
4. T I N K __ R
5. U M __ R E L L A
6. R O S __ T T A
7. I __ I D E S S A
8. F A I __ Y
9. M __ A
10. K A T __
11. __ T O R M

1	2	3	4	5	6	7	8	9	10	11

See page 244 for the answer.

Hide Out

What do Gabby and Iridessa sit in to stay dry when it rains? To find out, cross out all the letters in the word DRIP and write the remaining letters on the blanks below.

PIRADDIPHI

RPDPORDRL

IPDLIIRPDO

DDWRIDPL

DPPORIRIGIP

__ _____ ___

See page 244 for the answer.

Story Time

As they wait out the storm, Gabby tells Iridessa a story. Write your own story below:

Once upon a time, there was a _____

named_____

who lived in a place called _____

_____.

She/he was very_____

and loved to do all sorts of things such as

_____

and _____

_____.

One day she/he met a _____

_____.

Together, they_____

_____

_____

_____.

And they lived happily ever after.

Flower Power

Which path of dandelions will lead Gabby and Iridessa out of the forest?

A   B   C

See page 245 for the answer.

Surprise in the Sky

What do the girls see floating out of Gabby's bedroom window? Use the reverse alphabet code to find out.

WZMWVORLM

HVVWH

_ _ _ _ _ _ _ _ _ _

_ _ _ _ _

A = Z	
B = Y	
C = X	
D = W	
E = V	
F = U	
G = T	
H = S	
I = R	
J = Q	
K = P	
L = O	
M = N	
N = M	
O = L	
P = K	
Q = J	
R = I	
S = H	
T = G	
U = F	
V = E	
W = D	
X = C	
Y = B	
Z = A	

See page 245 for the answer.

Sisterly Love

Mia and Gabby are so happy to have found each other! How many times can you find the word SISTER in the puzzle below? Look up, down, across, backward, and diagonally.

```
R T R E T S I S
S R T S E I S T
I I E I T T I R
S I S T E R R E
T E R T R E S S
E S E S E T R I
R S I I S R T E
R T S I S T E R
```

See page 245 for the answer.

Back Home

Rosetta is thrilled to be back in Never Land!
Lead her through the maze to Tinker Bell.

See page 245 for the answer.

A New way IN

The portal between Never Land and the mainland has moved to Gabby's room! What does Iridessa say to Gabby? Unscramble the words to find out.

"VREEN DLNA UMTS ANTW UOY REEH."

"
_____ _____

_____ _____

____ _____."

See page 245 for the answer.

Pattern Path 3

Follow the pattern up, down, left, and right (but not diagonally) to make it through the puzzle. Follow this pattern!

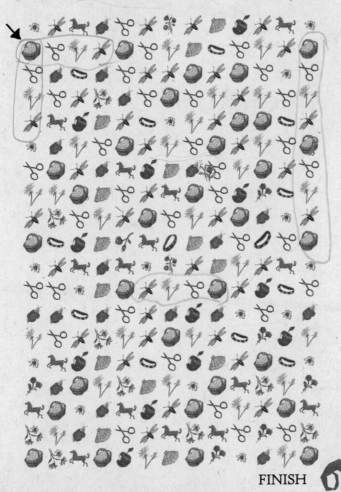

FINISH

See page 245 for the answer.

Mystery Map

Fill in the missing letters
to complete the map.

__ E V __ __
__ A __ __

__ I R __ T __
C __ __ E

T __ RT __
__ __ __ NT __ IN

S K __ __ __

P __ X __ __
R __ __ __

H __ __ __ __ W

M __ __ M __ __ D
__ A __ OO __

See page 246 for the answers.

Get wordy 3

How many words can you make using the letters in FROM THE MIST?

_____ _____

_____ _____

_____ _____

_____ _____

_____ _____

_____ _____

_____ _____

_____

_____

_____

_____

See page 246 for the answers.

Never Time

Time works differently in Never Land. Use the clues for ACROSS and DOWN to fill in the puzzle.

ACROSS

3. Sixty seconds
4. Sound a clock makes: _____-tock
5. Sixty minutes

DOWN

1. Set the _____.
2. Tall clock named for a relative

See page 246 for the answer.

Morning Mist

Gabby wakes up and discovers something strange. To find out what it is, replace each letter below with the one that comes after it in the alphabet.

"VGX HR LX

QNNL RN ENFFX?"

"___ __ __

____ __

_____?"

See page 246 for the answer.

An Old Fairy Saying

The letters below are scrambled, but they are in the correct columns. Rearrange the letters to find an old saying that Silvermist keeps thinking about.

F	A	I	O	I	E	S	N		T	A	K	E
W	I	S	N	I	I	G			T	H	E	
M	A	M	T	R	N		G			G		
		R	R		N	I	N					

See page 246 for the answer.

A Tangle of Silvermist

How many pictures of Silvermist can you count?

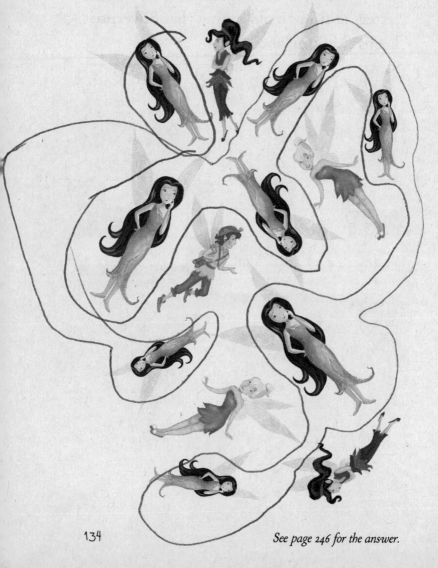

See page 246 for the answer.

Orders from the Queen

Follow the leaf code to see what Queen Clarion tells everyone about the mist.

See page 247 for the answer.

135

The Exception

The queen decides that some fairies should stay in the air as lookouts. To see which fairies are allowed to fly, cross out all the letters in the word FLY and write the remaining letters on the lines below.

YFLLTFYLHYLY

EFFYSLFYFCLL

YOFUTLYFLSF

___ ___ ___   ___ ___ ___ ___ ___ ___

See page 247 for the answer.

Wacky Weather

The wind is getting stronger! Unscramble the weather-related words. Then write the letters from the circles on the lines below to spell the unexpected sound everyone hears.

ONWS

□□□○

NETRHDU

□○□□□□□

MHIDU

□□□○□

INRA

□□□○

TGINNGLHI

□□□□□○○□□

LYCLIH

□□□□□○

___ ___ ___ ___ ___ ___ ___ ___

See page 247 for the answer.

Mist Horse Q & A

1. Where did everyone first see the mist horses?

    A) near the Home Tree

    B) in the meadow

    C) in the fairy circle

    D) up in the clouds

2. What color are the mist horses?

    A) purple

    B) black

    C) golden white

    D) silver white

3. Which girl rides a mist horse?

    A) Kate

    B) Mia

    C) Gabby

    D) Lainey

See page 247 for the answers.

Look Out Below!

Fawn gets flicked by a mist horse's tail. Find the path that will lead her safely to the ground.

A B C

See page 247 for the answer.

Pick your Horse

Which horse is different from the others?

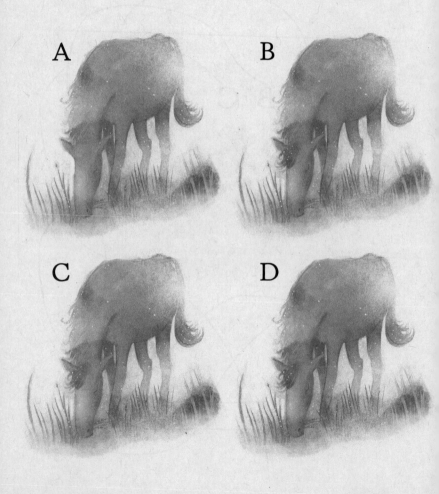

A

B

C

D

See page 247 for the answer.

Deep Thoughts

What do you suppose Kate is thinking about? Write your ideas here.

Design the Cover

Silvermist tries to find a book about the mist horse legend. What do you think the cover of the book would look like? Draw a picture, and don't forget to add a title!

Searching the Shelves

Lead Silvermist to the leaf-book.

See page 247 for the answer.

Book It!

To learn the title of the book Silvermist is reading, start at the arrow and, going counterclockwise, write every letter on the lines below.

↓

HAILSTONESINTHEHOLLOWANDTHEROADWEATHERFABLES

——— ——— ——— ——— ——— ——— ——— ——— ——— ——— ——— ——— ——— ———

——— ——— ___ ——— ——— ——— ——— ___ ——— ——— ——— ——— ——— ——— ———,

——— ——— ——— ___ ——— ——— ——— ——— ——— ___ ——— ——— ——— ———

——— ——— ——— ——— ——— ——— ——— ——— ———

——— ——— ——— ——— ——— ——— ———

See page 247 for the answer.

Just a Myth

Use the number code to reveal the myth of the mist horses.

20-8-5   8-15-18-19-5-19

5-14-3-8-1-14-20

20-8-5-9-18   18-9-4-5-18-19,

19-15   20-8-5-25

11-5-5-16   18-9-4-9-14-7

1-14-4   18-9-4-9-14-7.

___ _____

_____

_____

_____, __

____ ___

_____ ___

_____.

See page 247 for the answer.

A	= 1
B	= 2
C	= 3
D	= 4
E	= 5
F	= 6
G	= 7
H	= 8
I	= 9
J	= 10
K	= 11
L	= 12
M	= 13
N	= 14
O	= 15
P	= 16
Q	= 17
R	= 18
S	= 19
T	= 20
U	= 21
V	= 22
W	= 23
X	= 24
Y	= 25
Z	= 26

Animal Kingdom

Lots of animals live in Pixie Hollow. To find out what Kate names the mist horse, unscramble the animal names. Then write the letters from the circles on the lines below.

MPUICKHN

◯ ☐ ☐ ☐ ☐ ☐ ☐

ERRQLISU

☐ ☐ ☐ ☐ ☐ ☐ ☐ ◯

GOHGEHDE

☐ ☐ ☐ ☐ ☐ ◯ ☐

OSMUE

☐ ☐ ◯ ☐ ☐

REDE

◯ ☐ ☐ ☐

___ ___ ___ ___ ___

See page 248 for the answer.

Just Beachy

Kate and Cloud enjoy a ride on the beach.
Look up, down, across, and diagonally to
find these words in the puzzle.

DUNE OCEAN SEASHELL

SURF TIDE WAVES

```
H W A V E S O U F L
J A S D K Y L A R L
S L B W V G D U N E
U L O C Q M I N B H
R G E C S O L U I S
F T Y D E R Y F W A
W H I E M A P T D E
V A S D K O N J U S
F I O C E B I D R T
```

See page 248 for the answer.

Out Scouting

Lead Myka through the maze so she can tell Vidia that she's scouting for Kate and the lost fairies.

See page 248 for the answer.

Caught up

What does Kate lose as she swings herself free from the vines? To find out, follow the lines and write each letter in the correct box.

T R H T B E R A E R E

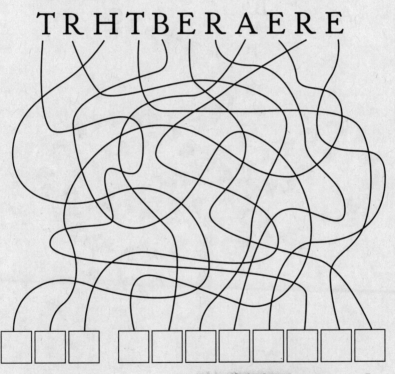

See page 248 for the answer.

Whose Hooves Are These?

Follow the trails of hoofprints. Which trail leads to the horse? Which one leads to the deer?

See page 248 for the answer.

Good Gabby

Circle the two pictures of Gabby that are exactly the same.

A

B

C

D

See page 248 for the answer.

That's No Rock!

Kate is surprised when what she thinks is a rock turns out to be a bear! How many times can you find the word BEAR in the puzzle below? Look up, down, across, backward, and diagonally.

```
B  B  B  E  A  R
E  A  E  R  R  B
A  B  A  A  R  E
R  B  R  E  R  R
B  A  B  E  R  A
A  B  E  R  A  E
R  A  E  B  R  B
```

See page 248 for the answer.

Kate's wish

The letters below are scrambled, but they are in the correct columns. Rearrange the letters to find out what Kate says to Cloud.

H	O	U	L	D	H	A	Y	W	M	Y	S
C	O	R	I	E		B	L	O	U	Y	
I		W	S	S		E		A			

Bear Talk

Lainey speaks in Mouse and the bear goes away. Start at the arrow and, going counterclockwise, write each letter on the lines below to find out what Silvermist says to Lainey.

" ___ ___ _____

_____ ___

_____ ___

_____ , _____

___ ' ___ _____ . _____ . "

See page 249 for the answer.

Mini Myka

Which shadow matches the picture of Myka exactly?

See page 249 for the answer.

See page 249 for the answer.

Gabby's Talent

Use the reverse alphabet code to see what Gabby says as she walks across the log.

"R'N Z YZOZMXV-GZOVMG UZRIB!"

"__ , __

_____-

_____

_____!"

A = Z
B = Y
C = X
D = W
E = V
F = U
G = T
H = S
I = R
J = Q
K = P
L = O
M = N
N = M
O = L
P = K
Q = J
R = I
S = H
T = G
U = F
V = E
W = D
X = C
Y = B
Z = A

Horse Trail

To reach the end of the puzzle, follow the path of horses that are pointing only to the right. You can move up, down, left, and right (but not diagonally).

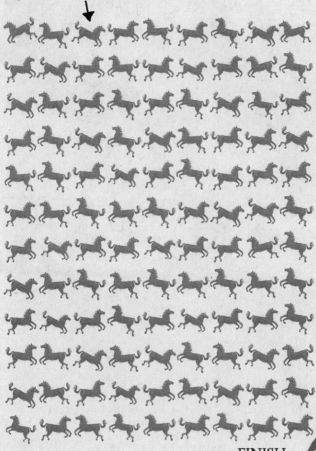

FINISH

See page 249 for the answer.

In Flight

Which two pictures are exactly alike?

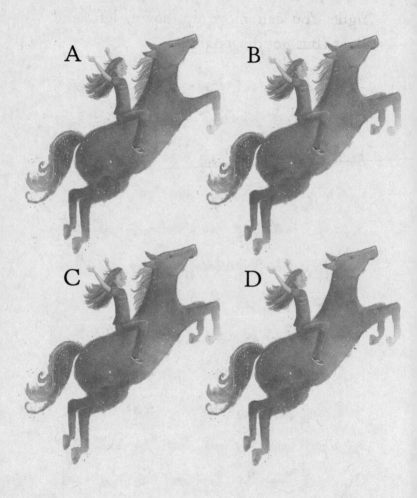

A

B

C

D

See page 249 for the answer.

Kate's Journey

Kate has quite an adventure with Cloud.
Which things did *not* happen?

1. Cloud was sprinkled with fairy dust.
2. Cloud hid in a cave.
3. Cloud ran down a sand dune.
4. Kate was stung by a bee.
5. Kate climbed a tree to jump on
   Cloud's back.

See page 249 for the answers.

Silvermist the Tracker

Silvermist and the girls go all over Never Land to find Kate. Look up, down, across, and diagonally to find the places in the puzzle.

BEACH   CANYON

GROVE   RIVER

```
H A G E V Y H B
C T E R S C B J
A B N U O Y S R
N I C M H V P E
Y A J R I V E R
O S B E A C H A
N V N R I G B O
```

See page 249 for the answer.

Pattern Path 4

Follow the pattern up, down, left, and right (but not diagonally) to make it through the maze. Follow this pattern!

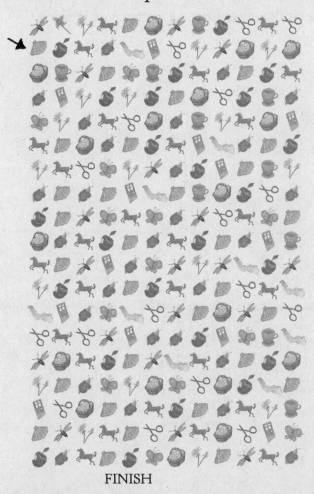

FINISH

See page 250 for the answer.

You're #1!

Every fairy in Pixie Hollow has a talent. It's the thing she does best and loves to do more than anything else. What is *your* special talent? Draw a picture of it here.

Fairy Dots

With a friend, take turns drawing a line to connect two dots below. When a line you draw completes a box, give yourself one point. If there's a fairy in the box, give yourself two points. When no more boxes can be made, the player with more points wins.

Play Again!

I Do!

Unscramble the wedding words.

DEBIR

— — — — —

OGOMR

— — — — —

NRIG

— — — —

ARRGMAEI

— — — — — — — —

EKCA

— — — —

WLESOFR

— — — — — — —

EASLI

— — — — —

OGNW

— — — —

See page 250 for the answers.

A = 1	
B = 2	
C = 3	
D = 4	
E = 5	
F = 6	
G = 7	
H = 8	
I = 9	
J = 10	
K = 11	
L = 12	
M = 13	
N = 14	
O = 15	
P = 16	
Q = 17	
R = 18	
S = 19	
T = 20	
U = 21	
V = 22	
W = 23	
X = 24	
Y = 25	
Z = 26	

Gabby's News

Use the number code to find what Gabby is excited about.

19-8-5   9-19

7-15-9-14-7   20-15

2-5   1

6-12-15-23-5-18

7-9-18-12

___ ___   ___ ___

___ ___ ___ ___ ___

___ ___   ___ ___   ___

___ ___ ___ ___ ___

___ ___ ___ ___.

166

See page 250 for the answer.

Here Comes the Bride

Who is getting married? To find out, replace each letter with the one that comes after it in the alphabet.

ITKHZ, FZAAX'R AZAXRHSSDQ

_ _ _ _ _ _ ,

_ _ _ _ _ _ _ _

_ _ _ _ _ _ _ _ _ _ _ _

See page 250 for the answer.

Petal Practice

Bess adds fairy dust to Gabby's flower petals so they'll float around a bit before falling to the ground. How many petals can you count?

See page 250 for the answer.

Fairy Magic

Who gives Gabby a thimble-sized bucket of fairy dust to use at the wedding? To find out, follow the lines and write each letter in the correct box.

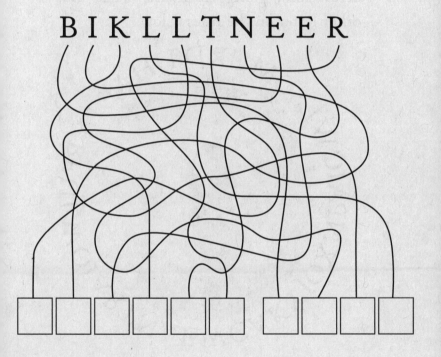

B I K L L T N E E R

Wedding Knowledge

Gabby tells her fairy friends about Clumsy weddings, but she gets some facts wrong. To find out what Gabby says the bride and groom do after the wedding, start at the arrow and, going clockwise, write every other letter on the lines below.

" ___ ___ ___ ___ ___   ___ ___ ___ ___ ___

___ ___ ___ ___ ___   ___ ___ ___   ___ ___

___ ___ ___ ___ ___ ___ . "

See page 250 for the answer.

Meet Bess

Which three statements about Bess are true?

1. Bess often keeps a pencil tucked behind her ear.
2. She has a pet iguana.
3. Bess is an art-talent fairy.
4. She once painted the Home Tree pink.
5. Bess sleeps in a banana peel.
6. Her easel is made out of matchsticks.

See page 250 for the answer.

Artist's Assistant

Bess painted this picture of a dew-covered spiderweb. Draw a spider or two to go with it.

All Dressed Up

Gabby is dressed for the wedding, but her mother tells her to take one thing off. To find out what, unscramble the words. Then write the letters from the circles on the line below.

WTEASRE

☐ ◯ ☐ ☐ ☐ ☐ ☐

ITSRH

☐ ☐ ◯ ☐ ☐

SPTAN

☐ ☐ ◯ ☐ ☐

TTISGH

☐ ☐ ◯ ☐ ☐ ☐

SEDRS

☐ ☐ ☐ ☐ ◯

Gabby is told to take off her

___ ___ ___ ___ ___ .

Surprise Visitor

Gabby is surprised to find Bess in her room. Connect the dots to see what the fairy squeezed through to get in.

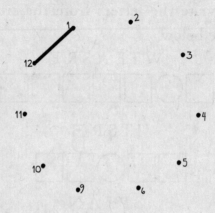

See page 251 for the answer.

A Basket of Bess

Which picture is different from the others?

A   B

C   D

E   F

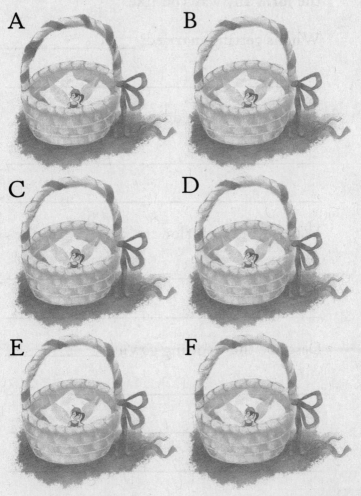

See page 251 for the answer.

The wedding Planner

Pretend you're planning a wedding. Fill out the form any way you like.

Who is getting married? _____

_____

Where will the wedding be held? _____

_____

_____

What kinds of flowers will be in the bride's bouquet? _____

_____

Describe the wedding gown: _____

_____

_____

_____

_____

Describe the bridesmaids' dresses: _____

_____

_____

_____

Describe the wedding cake: _____

_____

_____

What song will the happy couple dance to?

_____

_____

Where will they go on their honeymoon?

_____

_____

_____

_____

No Touching

Ms. Cork, the wedding planner, tells Gabby not to touch Julia's veil. How many times can you find the word VEIL in the puzzle? Look up, down, across, backward, and diagonally.

```
V E I L V V
L L L E I E
L V E I L I
V I V E I L
E E V V V L
I E I L E I
L I E L V E
I V E I L V
```

See page 251 for the answer.

Choose a word 4

Find the best word to complete each sentence.

LIGHT   COUCH   HEAD

SHELF   PATCH   BASKET

FLASH   HANGER   FOOTPRINT

1. Bess tells Gabby she'll be back in a

firefly's _____ .

2. The veil slides off the _____ .

3. Gabby puts the veil on her _____ .

4. Oh no! The veil has a _____

on it.

See page 251 for the answers.

Curious Bess

Which shadow matches the picture of Bess exactly?

See page 251 for the answer.

Follow That Veil!

Gabby puts fairy dust on the veil and it floats out the window! Follow the path of the veil  in any direction up through the puzzle, from the bottom to the top.

FINISH

Magic Words

What does Gabby say when she sprinkles the fairy dust? To find out, replace each letter with the one that comes before it in the alphabet.

BCSBDBEBCSB

" __ __ __ __ __ __ __ __ __ __ __ !"

See page 252 for the answer.

Extra Extra Large

Bess checks out the place settings at the wedding and is amazed by how huge everything is. A bowl could be her bathtub. A teaspoon could be a garden-talent's shovel. What could a fairy use the items listed below for? Write your ideas under each one.

OVEN MITT

_____

_____

_____

PENCIL

_____

_____

_____

COMB

_____

_____

_____

SHOELACE

_____

_____

_____

Mind Your Manners 4

Bess thinks she spots two fairies across the room and goes to greet them. What do fairies say to each other instead of "hello"? Use the leaf code to find out.

"＿ ＿ ＿   ＿ ＿ ＿ ＿   ＿ ＿ ＿!"

See page 252 for the answer.

Stuck!

What do Bess's feet get stuck in at the wedding? To find out, follow the lines and write each letter in the correct box.

S I F G N O T R

cake Artist

Decorate your own wedding cake.

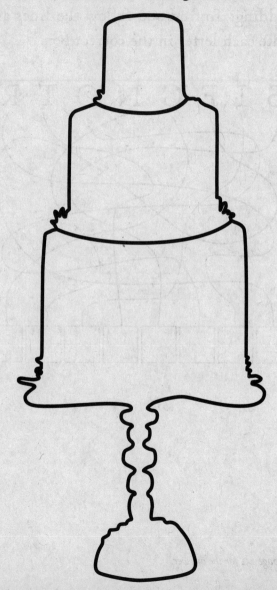

Yummy

Can you fit the words below into the puzzle?

CAKE   CHOCOLATE   CREAM

SUGAR   SWEET   VANILLA

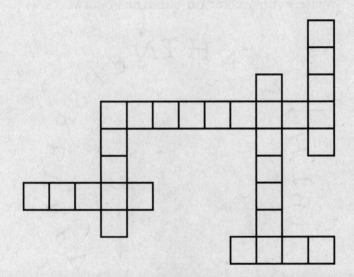

See page 252 for the answer.

Chocolate Fairy

After Bess falls into the chocolate fountain, she is spotted by an adult Clumsy. To find out what the Clumsy shouts, start at the arrow and, going counterclockwise, write every letter on the lines below.

" _ _ _ _ _ _ , _ _ _ _

_ _ _ _ _ _ _ _ _

_ _ _ _ _ _ ' _ _

_ _ _ _ _ _ _ _ _ _ ! "

See page 252 for the answer.

The Ring Bearer

A boy Gabby's age is also in the wedding. To learn his name, cross out all the letters in the word BOY and write the remaining letters on the lines below.

OYBYDBOOAY

BNBYOOBIYO

YYEBLBYOOBB

_ _ _ _ _ _

See page 252 for the answer.

Bug Collector

Daniel's favorite bug is a dragonfly. Unscramble the bug words. Then write the letters in the circles on the lines below to complete the sentence.

OHCRCKAOC

☐ ☐ ☐ ◯ ☐ ☐ ☐ ☐

ACDACI

☐ ◯ ☐ ☐ ☐ ☐

TMEERIT

◯ ☐ ☐ ☐ ☐ ☐ ☐

EETBEL

☐ ◯ ☐ ☐ ☐ ☐

Daniel wants to fly his

___ ___ ___ ___ .

See page 252 for the answer.

Flower Girl Dash

Help Gabby catch up with the flying veil.

See page 252 for the answer.

Look-Alikes

Which two pictures of Bess are exactly alike?

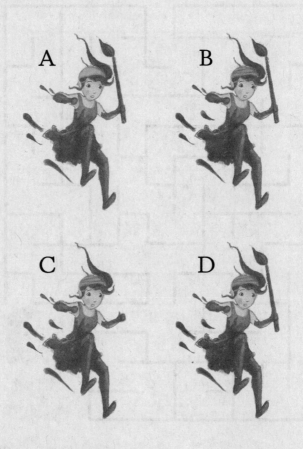

See page 253 for the answer.

Caught!

Daniel puts Bess in a bag, thinking she's a bug. Connect the dots to see what he gives her to eat.

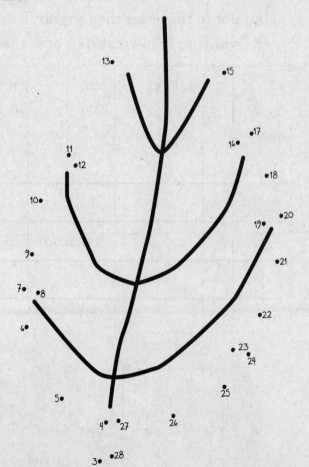

See page 253 for the answer.

193

Snack in a Sack

Bess is hungry, but she doesn't want to eat food fit for a bug. The words in each vertical column go into spaces directly below them, but not in the order they appear. Rearrange the words to read what Bess does instead.

BIT	BREAKS	AND	NIBBLES
ON	IT	OFF	COVERING
HER	OF		
SHE			A
		CHOCOLATE	
	BODY		

See page 253 for the answer.

The Chase Continues

The veil is still out of reach. What does Gabby do to try to get closer to it? Use the reverse alphabet code to find out.

HSV

HKIRMPOVH UZRIB

WFHG LM SVIHVOU

ZMW UORVH

_ _ _

_ _ _ _ _ _ _ _ _

_ _ _ _ _ _ _ _ _ _ _ _

_ _ _ _ _ _ _ _ _

_ _ _ _ _ _ _ _ .

A = Z
B = Y
C = X
D = W
E = V
F = U
G = T
H = S
I = R
J = Q
K = P
L = O
M = N
N = M
O = L
P = K
Q = J
R = I
S = H
T = G
U = F
V = E
W = D
X = C
Y = B
Z = A

See page 253 for the answer.

Surprise in the Sky

These words are all things you wouldn't expect to fly. Look up, down, across, backward, and diagonally to find them in the puzzle.

CAT   GABBY   OSTRICH

PENGUIN   WHALE

```
Y B H N I W S O
H P Z G A B B Y
C L E D T O E T
I J A N C W D I
R B S E G P B L
T A C J T U A A
S P E K M S I Y
O N W H A L E N
```

See page 253 for the answer.

Treetop Rescue

Gabby needs help. Which path leads to her?

A   B   C

See page 253 for the answer.

Tree Scramble

Gabby gets stuck in a willow tree.
Unscramble these other tree names.

NPIE

__ __ __ __

MPLA

__ __ __ __

PLPAE

__ __ __ __ __

KOA

__ __ __

AMLPE

__ __ __ __ __

OELNM

__ __ __ __ __

RFI

__ __ __

EML

__ __ __

RRYCEH

__ __ __ __ __ __

RIHCB

__ __ __ __ __

See page 254 for the answers.

The Pixie Hollow Rule

What is the rule that all the girls agreed on—and that Gabby has broken more than once? Use the number code to find out.

20-15 1-12-23-1-25-19

7-15 20-15 16-9-24-9-5

8-15-12-12-15-23

20-15-7-5-20-8-5-18

___ ___ ___ ___ ___ ___ ___ ___

___ ___ ___ ___ ___

___ ___ ___ ___ ___

___ ___ ___ ___ ___ ___

___ ___ ___ ___ ___ ___ ___ ___

| A = 1 |
| B = 2 |
| C = 3 |
| D = 4 |
| E = 5 |
| F = 6 |
| G = 7 |
| H = 8 |
| I = 9 |
| J = 10 |
| K = 11 |
| L = 12 |
| M = 13 |
| N = 14 |
| O = 15 |
| P = 16 |
| Q = 17 |
| R = 18 |
| S = 19 |
| T = 20 |
| U = 21 |
| V = 22 |
| W = 23 |
| X = 24 |
| Y = 25 |
| Z = 26 |

See page 254 for the answer.

Bird's-Eye View

What does Gabby see while holding on to Daniel's kite? To find out, go from left to right and write all the letters on the lines below.

CAROU
SELPO
NDBAL
LFIEL
DTENT

__ __ __ __ __ __ __ __

__ __ __ __

__ __ __ __ __ __ __ __ __ __

__ __ __ __ __

See page 254 for the answers.

Create a Kite

Decorate the kite any way you like.

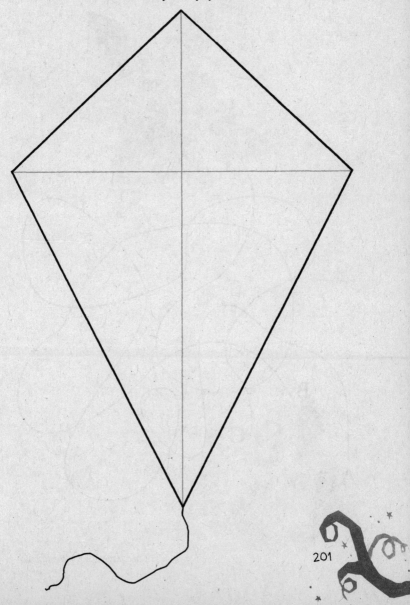

Hold On!

Which string is attached to the kite?

A

B

C

See page 254 for the answer.

Extra Guests

More fairies have come to the wedding. Can you fit their names into the puzzle?

BESS   DULCIE   PRILLA

ROSETTA   SILVERMIST   TINK

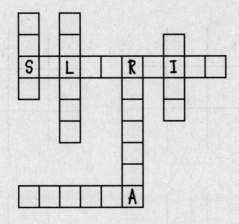

See page 254 for the answer.

Wedding Tic-Tac-Toe

Find a friend to play with you. Instead of X's and O's, one of you will be hearts ♥ and the other will be rings ⊙.

Take turns and draw your symbol in one of the nine tic-tac-toe squares. If you get three of your symbols in a row horizontally, vertically, or diagonally, you win!

♥ Play Some More! 💍

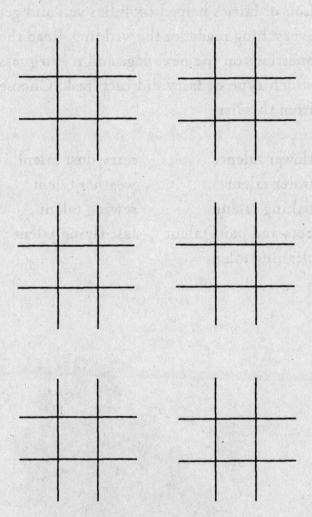

Fairies to the Rescue

Lots of fairies helped fix Julia's veil and get everything ready for the wedding. Read the questions on the next page and try to guess which type of fairy did each task. Choose from this list:

flower talent
water talent
baking talent
pots-and-pans talent
cleaning talent

fairy-dust talent
weather talent
sewing talent
fast-flying talent

1. Who stitched up the hole in the veil?

_____

2. Who got rid of the stains on the veil?

_____

3. Who added dewdrops to the veil to

make it sparkle? _____

_____

4. Who collected flower petals for Gabby's

basket? _____

_____

5. Who smoothed out the frosting on the

wedding cake? _____

_____

See page 254 for the answers.

Ready to Wed

What does Julia say when she finally puts her veil on? To find out, start at the arrow and, going clockwise, write every other letter on the lines below. ↓

" _ _ _ _   _ _ _ _   _ _ _ _ _ _ _ _

_ _ _ _   _   _ _ _ _ _ _ _ _ . "

See page 254 for the answer.

Wedding Day True-or-False

Which statements are true and which ones are false?

1. Gabby wore her wings during the wedding.

    True

    False

2. Bess sat on the groom's head.

    True

    False

3. Gabby hopped down the aisle.

    True

    False

4. The wedding cake was lemon with vanilla cream.

    True

    False

5. Julia tripped on her veil as she danced.

    True

    False

See page 254 for the answers.

Cake Dots

With a friend, take turns drawing a line to connect two dots below. When a line you draw completes a box, give yourself one point. If there's a slice of cake in the box, give yourself two points. When no more boxes can be made, the player with more points wins.

Play Again!

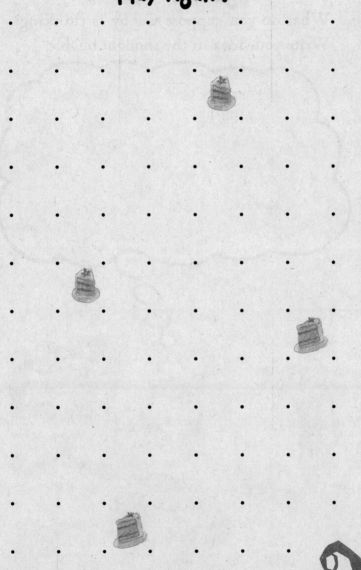

Delightful Daydream

What do you suppose Gabby is thinking?
Write your idea in the thought bubble.

A New Friend

Gabby introduces Daniel to the fairies. Fill in the missing letters to see what he says to Bess.

"__OR__Y I P__T

Y__ __ IN A B__ __.

I TH__ __GHT __OU

W__R__ A __ __G."

See page 255 for the answer.

Painting Time

Bess uses a napkin as a canvas and paints some wedding scenes. Draw your own versions in the frames.

Gabby Throwing Flower Petals

The Bride in Her Veil

The Happy Groom

The Fairies

A = 1
B = 2
C = 3
D = 4
E = 5
F = 6
G = 7
H = 8
I = 9
J = 10
K = 11
L = 12
M = 13
N = 14
O = 15
P = 16
Q = 17
R = 18
S = 19
T = 20
U = 21
V = 22
W = 23
X = 24
Y = 25
Z = 26

Masterpiece

What does Gabby suggest they do with Bess's painting? Use the number code to find out.

12-5-1-22-5　9-20　23-9-20-8

20-8-5　15-20-8-5-18

16-18-5-19-5-14-20-19

6-15-18　10-21-12-9-1

1-14-4　8-5-18

8-21-19-2-1-14-4

___ ___ ___ ___ ___ ___ ___ ___ ___ ___ ___ ___ ___

___ ___ ___ ___ ___ ___ ___ ___ ___ ___

___ ___ ___ ___ ___ ___ ___ ___ ___ ___ ___ ___ ___ ___ ___

___ ___ ___ ___ ___ ___ ___ ___ ___ ___ ___

___ ___ ___ ___ ___ ___ ___ ___ ___ ___ ___ ___ ___ .

216

See page 255 for the answer.

Get wordy 4

How many words can you make from the letters in "THE NEVER GIRLS"?

_____   _____

_____   _____

_____   _____

_____   _____

_____   _____

_____   _____

See page 255 for the answers.

Shadow Matching

Match each fairy to her shadow.

PRILLA ___

TINKER BELL ___

SILVERMIST ___

BESS ___

QUEEN CLARION ___

ROSETTA ___

See page 255 for the answers.

Fairy Descriptions

Which fairy does each statement describe?

1. She has pom-poms on her shoes.

_____

2. She lives in a sour plum tree.

_____

3. She has a long braid.

_____

4. She wears a thin band of gold on her

head. _____

5. Her glow is stronger than that of most

fairies. _____

See page 255 for the answers.

Girl Talk

Which Never Girl does each statement describe?

1. She loves to play sports and climb trees.

_____

2. She wears glasses.

_____

3. She has a big dollhouse.

_____

4. She believes that fairies can grant

wishes. _____

See page 255 for the answers.

You're a Fairy!

What kind of fairy would you like to be?
Use your imagination and fill in the blanks.

Your fairy name: _____

_____

Your fairy talent: _____

_____

Describe your fairy outfit: _____

_____

_____

_____

How would you decorate your room in the

Home Tree? _____

_____

_____

_____

What fairy food would you most like
to eat? _____

_____

_____

Which fairies would you most want to be

friends with? _____

_____

_____

Draw a picture of yourself as a fairy!

A Special Journey

There are two ways to reach Never Land.
Use the leaf code to discover them.

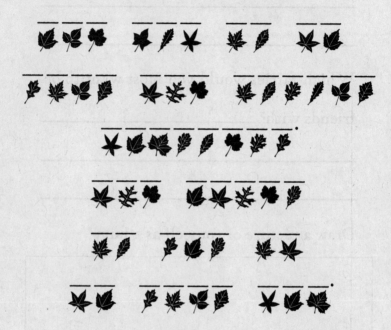

See page 255 for the answer.

Silly Grown-ups

Why can't most grown-ups see fairies? To find out, replace each letter with the one that comes before it in the alphabet.

ZPV DBO'U TFF

GBJSJFT JG

ZPV EPO'U

CFMJFWF JO UIFN.

____ ___'_

___ _____

__ ___ ___'_

_____ __

_____.

See page 256 for the answer.

Best of the Best

Write a review for each Never Girls chapter book. Say what you like about each book and give each one a rating from 1 to 5 stars. (Five stars means it's your fairy favorite!)

_____

_____

_____

_____

_____

_____

_____

_____

_____

_____

_____

_____

_____

_____

_____

_____

_____

_____

_____

_____

_____

_____

_____

_____

_____

_____

_____

_____

_____

_____

_____

_____

_____

_____

_____

_____

_____

_____

The Next Chapter

Create your own cover for a future Never Girls chapter book. Don't forget to include a title!

Four real girls in a fairy's world.

Disney

The Never Girls

Kiki Thorpe

illustrated by Jana Christy

Fairies Forever!

How many times can you find the word FAIRY in the puzzle? Look up, down, across, backward, and diagonally.

```
Y R I A F Y F A
R I A Y R I A F
I Y F F I R I R
A I R A A I R F
F R I I I A Y A
F F Y R F R F I
A A Y Y A F Y R
I I I F A I R Y
R R A R I A F R
Y Y F A Y I R Y
```

See page 256 for the answers.

Answers

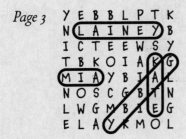

Page 3

Y E B B L P T K
N L A I N E Y B
I C T E E W S Y
T B K O I A K G
M I A Y B I A L
N O S C G B T N
L W G M B I E G
E L A Y K M O L

Page 4
1) A; 2) C; 3) D

Page 5
"Clap if you believe in fairies!"

Page 6
Clumsies

Page 8
A teakettle

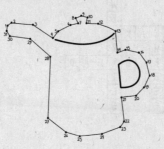

Page 9
Peter Pan

Page 11

Page 12
Welcome to Pixie Hollow.

Page 13

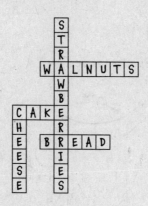

Page 14
1) Home; 2) rose; 3) blink; 4) tutu

Cute; Fairies think it's insulting to be called cute.

"I'd fly backward if I could."

C

1) B; 2) D; 3) C

B and E

1, 3, 6

Fireflies

Come to the fairy circle.

Page 27
Toadstool

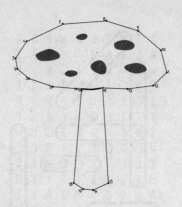

Page 28
A

Page 29
"We want to learn to fly."

Page 30
1) A; 2) C; 3) B

Page 31

Page 33
A fast-flying fairy.

Page 34
A sock

Page 35
butterfly, fairy, kite, airplane, helicopter.
The sparrow man's name is Terence.

Page 36

Page 37
Starling

Page 38
1) B; 2) C; 3) A

Page 39
"Fly safely!"

Page 40

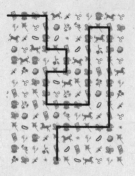

Page 42

Some possible answers: ace, act, ant, ante, ape, asp, ate, awe, base, bat, bath, bathe, beach, beast, beat, beet, bent, best, cab, can, cane, cap, cape, cast, cat, each, ease, east, eat, ewe, hat, hate, heap, heat, pace, pact, past, paste, pat, pest, pet, sap, sat, seat, seen, sew, sewn, shape, she, spa, spat, speech, spew, tap, tape, tease, teen, ten, tense, tent, tween, wasp, waste, web, west, wet, what.

Page 43
C

Page 44

Page 45
"You're becoming a real animal-talent Clumsy."

Page 48
B

Page 49
Mia, B; Kate, D; Gabby, A; Lainey, C

Page 50
One pinch of fairy dust each

Page 51
10

Page 52
Look for the second star to the right and fly
straight on till morning.

Page 54
6 times

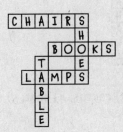

Page 56

Page 57
"Don't be so grouchy. I'm your friend."

Page 58
A broom

Page 59

Page 60
1) D; 2) B; 3) D

Page 61
1) bells; 2) brush; 3) fence; 4) shoe

Page 62
bird; dragonfly

Page 63

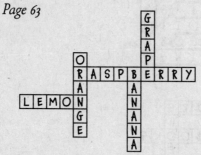

Page 64
1) chat; 2) escalator; 3) cactus; 4) coat; 5) scatter;
6) catcher

Page 65

Page 68
pots and pans; peppercorns

Page 69
He has a notch in his ear.

Page 70
waffle

Page 71
"Don't you think it's strange that a Never Land
mouse turned up in my home?"

Page 72

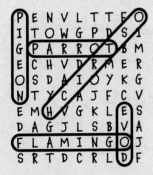

Page 73

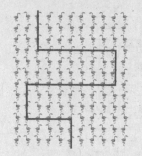

Page 74
rose, daisy, petunia, tulip, marigold

Page 75
"I swear on my wings, I was *inches* from being eaten!"

Page 76
B and D

Page 78

Page 79
the butterfly net; E

Page 80
1) paw; 2) swim; 3) wings

Page 81
her slingshot

Page 82

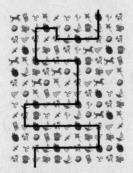

Page 83
She tugs on her bangs.

Page 86
Some possible answers: ail, ale, and, ash, awl, dale, deal, den, dew, dial, dine, dined, dish, done, end, eon, had, hand, head, heal, hen, his, howl, idle, idol, ion, lad, land, lash, law, lead, lean, led, lid, lie, lied, lion, new, nod, nine, ode, oil, one, owl.

Page 88
Mami and Papi

Page 90

Page 91
"We think Bingo must have smashed it when he was chasing fairies."

Page 92

1) C; 2) D; 3) F; 4) E; 5) B; 6) A

Page 93

Numbers 2, 3, and 5 are true.

Page 96

1) bread; 2) bleed; 3) bead; 4) robbed; 5) slobbered

Page 97

1) canopy bed; 2) dresser; 3) couch; 4) oven;
5) lamp; 6) table; 7) pillow; 8) chair; 9) curtain;
10) rug

Page 98

Page 99

Gabby's sweatshirt

Page 100

Rosetta is stuck on the mainland.
Gabby is stuck in Never Land.

Page 101

C

Page 102

Page 103
"The portal has vanished!"

Page 104
She faints.

Page 105
Cracker

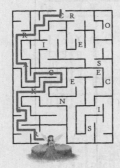

Page 106
1) C; 2) A; 3) C

Page 107
A fairy hears your wish and makes it come true.

Pages 108-109
A storm

Page 110

Page 111
Mrs. Peavy

Page 112
"Flowers need love and care. You can't just ignore them."

Page 114

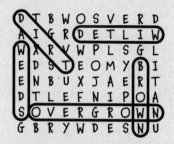

Page 115

Page 116
"It's louder than a bullfrog with a bellyache!"

Page 117
D

Page 118
1) Gabby; 2) Lainey; 3) queen; 4) tinker;
5) umbrella; 6) Rosetta; 7) Iridessa; 8) fairy;
9) Mia; 10) Kate; 11) storm; blueberries

Page 119
A hollow log

Page 122
A

Page 123
dandelion seeds

Page 124
5 times

Page 125

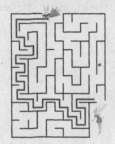

Page 126
"Never Land must want you here."

Page 127

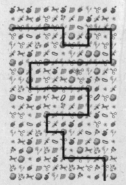

Page 130

Some possible answers: fir, fire, first, fist, for, form, fort, frost, hem, her, him, hire, his, hit, host, hot, ire, met, mime, mitt, mom, more, set, sit, soft, softer, stem, them, time, timer, tore.

Page 131

Page 132

"Why is my room so foggy?"

Page 133

Mist in the morning, fairies take warning.

Page 134

8

Page 135
"It's too dangerous to fly in weather like this.
So for now, all fairies are grounded."

Page 136
the scouts

Page 137
snow, thunder, humid, rain, lightning, chilly; whinny

Page 138
1) B; 2) D; 3) A

Page 139
C

Page 140
A

Page 143

Page 144
Hailstones in the Hollow, and Other Odd Weather Fables

Page 145
The horses enchant their riders, so they keep
riding and riding.

Page 146

chipmunk, squirrel, hedgehog, mouse, deer; Cloud

Page 147

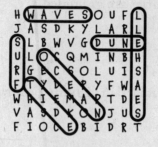

Page 148

Page 149

her barrette

Page 150

B and C

Page 151

B and D

Page 152

7 times

Page 153
"I wish you could be my horse, always."

Page 154
"He probably thought you were the biggest mouse he'd ever seen."

Page 155
B

Page 156
"I'm a balance-talent fairy!"

Page 157

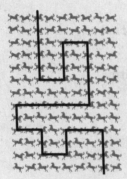

Page 158
B and C

Page 159
Numbers 1 and 2 did not happen.

Page 160

Page 161

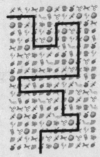

Page 165
bride, groom, ring, marriage, cake, flowers, aisle, gown

Page 166
She is going to be a flower girl.

Page 167
Julia, Gabby's babysitter

Page 168
39

Page 169
Tinker Bell

Page 170
"They float away on a cloud."

Page 171
Numbers 1, 3, and 6 are true.

Page 173
sweater, shirt, pants, tights, dress; wings

Page 174
a keyhole

Page 175
A

Page 178
8 times

Page 179
1) flash; 2) hanger; 3) head; 4) footprint

Page 180
C

Page 181

251

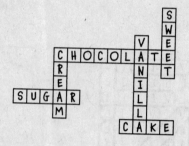

Page 192
B and D

Page 193
a leaf

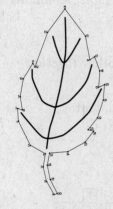

Page 194
She breaks off a bit of chocolate covering her body and nibbles on it.

Page 195
She sprinkles fairy dust on herself and flies.

Page 196

Page 197
B

Page 198

pine, palm, apple, oak, maple, lemon, fir, elm, cherry, birch

Page 199

To always go to Pixie Hollow together

Page 200

carousel, pond, ball field, tent

Page 202

B

Page 203

Pages 206–207

1) sewing talent; 2) cleaning talent;
3) water talent; 4) flower talent; 5) baking talent

Page 208

"It's even prettier than I remembered."

Page 209

1) true; 2) false; 3) false; 4) true; 5) false

Page 213
"Sorry I put you in a bag. I thought you were a bug."

Page 216
Leave it with the other presents for Julia and her husband.

Page 217
Some possible answers: eve, even, ever, gene, genie, gent, get, green, grin, grit, hen, her, his, hit, leg, lever, line, lint, listen, lit, live, liver, net, nit, rig, rile, rite, seven, sign, sing, singer, stern, sting, stinger, tee, teen, ten, then, these, this, tiger, tile, tire.

Pages 218-219
A) Prilla; B) Queen Clarion; C) Bess;
D) Silvermist; E) Rosetta; F) Tinker Bell

Page 220
1) Tinker Bell; 2) Vidia; 3) Fawn;
4) Queen Clarion; 5) Iridessa

Page 221
1) Kate; 2) Lainey; 3) Mia; 4) Gabby

Page 224
One way is to find the island yourself.
The other is for it to find you.

Page 225

You can't see fairies if you don't believe in them.

Page 230

11 times

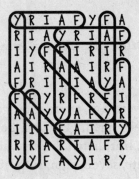